For Albie, Jake and Edwin.

The Cockchafer, colloquially know as the May Bug or Doodle Bug.

In a garden sat in dewy grass,
Was a boy with auburn hair.
On his nose a splash of freckles,
And his skin was very fair.

He sat there with his action man,
When much to his surprise,
The BIGGEST BLOOMING BEETLE,
Scuttled right before his eyes.

This was no common beetle,
He had seen some different types.
This one was HUGE and reddish brown,
With cool go faster stripes.

It had white teeth like bunting,
Running down both of its sides.
A funny little furry face,
And big black bulging eyes.

He took it to his mother,
Who failed a calm approach.
"GET IT OUT! You silly boy,
I think it's a cockroach!"

He went to show his sister,
She was writing in her jotter.
"TAKE THAT THING AWAY!" She shrieked,
"You nasty little rotter!"

He knocked on the door of his brothers room,
For he was very clever.
"I've told you Squirt, get out of here,
You're banned from here... FOREVER!"

The boy, quite sad, thought for a while,
"I'll take it to my Dad,
He'll not be so scared of it,
Or get so very mad."

So, he went to ask his Daddy
"It's a Cockchafer…I think."
The boy thought: WHAT A BUG I've found,
It's made my Dad turn pink!!!

Though of his father's answer,
He wasn't quite so sure.
So, he crept along to Granny's room,
And knocked upon the door.

Since breakfast Gran had not been seen,
Complaining indigestion.
The boy knew deep inside his heart,
She'd answer him his question.

She saw the young boys freckled face,
Her eyes were all a twinkle.
She smiled a kindly toothy grin,
To exaggerate each wrinkle.

"Come dear boy, what have you there,
For your old Gran to inspect?"
"A beetle Gran, a MASSIVE one,
The most enormous insect!"

"My boy what you have brought to me
Sat with you on my rug,
Is no ordinary beetle,
It's a magic Doodle Bug!"

"You must make a wish young chap,
It's true you mark my words.
Your wish is sure to happen,
As the singing of the birds."

So, he'd found a magic Doodle Bug,
And wished for what he'd like,
The best thing HE could think of,
Was a bright red racer bike.

His teeth were clean, he climbed the stairs
And snuggled into bed,
With thoughts of bugs and racer bikes
Zooming round his head.

He must have drifted off to sleep,
It didn't take him long,
But when he woke he realised,
His Doodle Bug was GONE!!

His Gran stretched out her sagging arms,
And offered him a hug.
"There, there my boy, I'll help you find
Your magic Doodle Bug."

Then came a knocking at the door,
Dad stood and scratched his head…

… "Just who'd leave us a present??
IT'S A RACER BIKE IN RED!!!?"

This publication was printed sustainably in the UK by Pureprint, a CarbonNeutral® company with FSC® chain of custody and an ISO 14001 certified environmental management system recycling over 99% of all dry waste.

Designed by freuds Branded

ISBN 9781916484238